Nine Men Chase a Hen

Written by
Barbara Gregorich

Illustrated by
John Sandford

One hen wants a hat.

Two men laugh at that.

Three men have a pet.

Four hens get very wet.

Five hens write a letter.

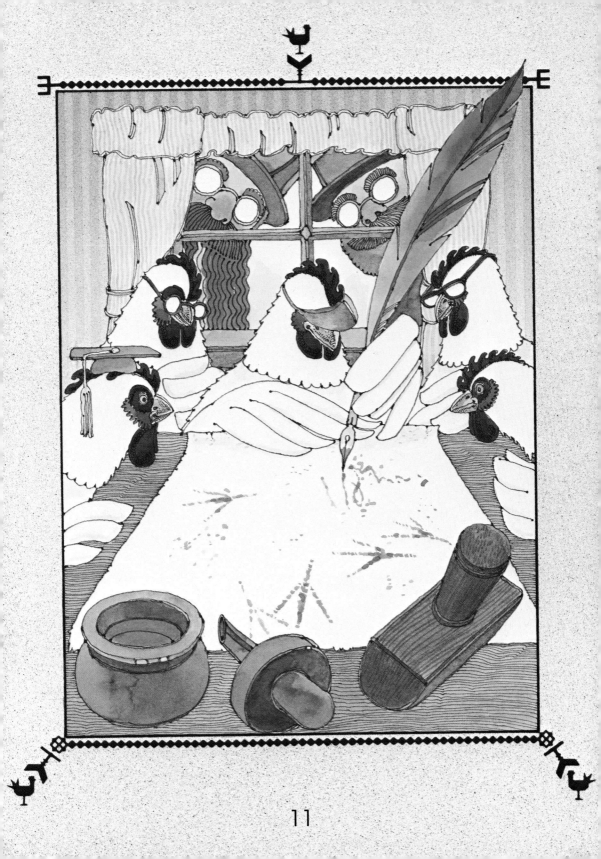

Six men say theirs is better.

Seven men sleep at night.

Eight hens make it light.

Nine men chase a hen.

Ten hens chase the men.

All the men run away.

All the hens begin to play.

25

Now this funny story ends.

All the men and hens are friends.

The End